DRIBBLES
DRABBLES
AND
POSTCARDS

An anthology of short, short stories

collected
and edited
by Darcy Nybo

Copyright 2022 © Darcy Nybo

All rights reserved. No part of this publication may be reproduced, stored in a retrieval system, or transmitted, in any form, or by any means (electronic, mechanical, photocopying, recording or otherwise) without prior written permission.

For book signings and wholesale enquiries please email darcy@alwayswrite.ca

ISBN 978-1-987982-60-2 (Paperback)
ISBN 978-1-987982-62-6 (Hardcover)
ISBN 978-1-987982-61-9 (eBook)

First Edition

Collected by Darcy Nybo
Cover by Darcy Nybo
Book Design by Artistic Warrior

This collection was gathered from writers from all over the world of all ages and backgrounds. Some are works of fiction, others are reported to be true. You decide which is which. For the fiction pieces, any similarity to people living or dead is entirely coincidental.

Artistic Warrior
A division of Always Write
https://alwayswrite.ca

An anthology of short, short stories

This book is dedicated to
every single writer out there
who keeps going until they get
it right. It takes courage to write
what's in your head and
share it with the world.
Thank you all for entertaining
us throughout the years.

Foreword 1

Dribbles: 50 Word Stories 3
A Simple Love Story 4
Attacked 5
The Mouth 6
Guilty 7
In Whirls of Darkness..8
Cast Black 9
Work 10
The Perfect Pitch 11
Liberating Death 12
A Sigh of Welcome 13
Duck 'n Gnome 14
Michele Rule 14
Patronized 15
Out of the Closet 16
Waters Run Deep 17
Work like a Dog 18
Epic 19
The Siren 20
The Robert Frost Murder 21
Flames of Fear 22
Drops 23
The Dolls 24
It Started Slowly 25
Plan Ahead 26
Begin Again...27
Sally's Song 28
The Man in Black 29
The Man 30
Imposter Syndrome 31
The Ceremony 32
The Attack 33

An anthology of short, short stories

Drabbles: 100 Word Stories..34
  The Importance of Charitable Support......................35
  Princess 36
  Shhh 37
  Breaking News! 38
  The Boy Who Lived in the Forest 39
  Go, Go, Stop!...40
  A Good Impression 41
  Space Delicacies 42
  Services Rendered 43
  Commercial Jingles Of a Certain Vintage 44
  The Ache 45
  A Night's Endeavour 46
  Beneath the Surface..47
  My Beloved, Humanity's Bane 48
  Lost..49
  Of Love and Legacies 50
  The Tyrant..51
  Skip the Carnage 52
  The Winner 53
  Doing Bach..54
  In the Widow's Garden 55
  Overkill 56
  The Dawn 57
  Nowhere to Hide 58
  Germs 59
  Maggie's Map 60
  Kidnapped 61
  Battle at Sunrise 62
  Together, Not Forever 63
  Sleep Tight..64
  Finding Dudley..65
  Fortune Cookie 66
  First Wife 67
  Sue...68
  Photograph 69

Dribbles, Drabbles, and Postcards

The Lottery Winner 70
White Linen Lady 71
Mary's Coffee 72
No More 73

Postcards: 240-250 Word Stories 74
The Lake 75
Strange Brew 77
The Funeral 79
New Traditions 81
Tale of a Mason Jar 83
Definitely Not Haunted 85
From the Highway, the River
Looks like a Grand Slam Breakfast for Dinner 87
Bird Strike 89
Karen and Carl...91
Deadlines 93
Moment with a Stranger 95
Leaving the Library in the Rain.............................97
Schoolyard Bricks and Mortar...............................99
The Presents 101
Cliff Hanger...103
Hello and Goodbye 105
You Grew Taller...107
Winter Wind 109
Risk 111
First Day of School 113
The Farmer 115
Hope 117
Sidestep 119
Fried Banana...121
The Big Score 123
Cell Phone Widow 125
Pigeon Post 127
The Following 129
One Last Ride 131

Mojave Mambo 133
A Nice Cup of Tea 135
Rest Area Intrigue 137
Sudden Storm 139
Fate 141
Dumpster Dave..143
A Renaissance Studio 145
Come Play with Me 147
Hard to Understand 149
The Cabin 151
Academic Priorities..153
The Sale 155
Silent Reverie 157
The Game 159

Author Biographies 161
Airth, Cathy 162
Agustín, Nelson 162
Boghean, Sue...162
Brown, Marilyn J. 163
Brown, P. F. 163
Buchan-Kimmerly, Elizabeth 163
Carr, Fern G. Z. 163
Cavouras, Anna 164
Clifton, Kristi..164
Corps, Tess 164
Gugin Maddex, Elaine.......................................165
Harris, Eileen 165
Hartley, Corina 165
Hartman, Christy 166
Jackson, Maggie...166
Jameson, Elaine 166
Johnson, Jo-Anne 167
Kierulf, Jackie 167
Kishchuk, Nat 167
Lancaster, Sharon 168

Leinemann, Theresa 168
Lewis, Marlene 168
Long-Shimanke, Mary 169
McNeill, Sharlene.. 169
Manchur, Jan 169
Minnings, Anne 170
Nybo, Darcy 170
Pawlik, Kelly 170
Platts-Fanning, Jennifer... 171
Quon, Sally.. 171
Ragaire, Hazel 171
Rebrec, Angela 171
Reilly, Katherine... 172
Robinson, Kathy 172
Rudolph, Diane 173
Rule, Michele 173
Scott, Larry 173
Seabrook, Kara 173
Smith, Kathy A. 174
Stephens, Dr. Margaret Editha aka Stevi Stephens 174
Stone, Rania... 175
Tiplady, Ann 175
Vollbrecht, Debby 175

Acknowledgements..176

Foreword

I love words, I love writing, and I love stories. Not long ago, I came upon the words dribble and drabble and was immediately struck by the amount of skill it would take to write a story that was exactly fifty (dribble) or one hundred words (drabble). I looked online to see if I could find any collections of these stories so I could read them and learn from them. I couldn't find anything, so I decided to create an anthology of them.

As a creative writing instructor, I am blessed to have hundreds of students who love to write and love a challenge. At first, I put out a call for submissions to only past students. Then I decided to open it up to the world. That is what you will read here. You'll find stories from people from every walk of life, age, and location.

In these pages, you'll find a wide variety of genres, writing styles, and topics. They have been chosen by a panel of judges.

The book is divided into three sections: dribbles, drabbles, and postcard short stories.

There was no set genre, and fiction is mixed in with non-fiction. There's also a section with author bios. Should you find an author you like, read their bio and, if they've supplied contact info, let them know.

Some of the stories may make you smile. Some may have you questioning humanity. Others may have you sleeping with the light on. We hope you find a few you really enjoy.

It takes some level of talent to be able to write a story with very few words.

On behalf of myself and all the writers in this book, we thank you for taking the time to read these snippets of storytelling.

We hope you find a few delightful tales to make your day just a little bit better and brighter.

An anthology of short, short stories

Dribbles: 50 Word Stories

A Simple Love Story
Tess Corps

I fear I am losing my balance, as I am already struggling.

Then came you …

And now I know to lose my balance, for our love is part of living a balanced life.

Because everything I went through, every bad relationship or experience, was only paving the way towards you.

Attacked
Larry Scott

The searing pain was deepening by the second.

Who would shoot me in the hand with a BB gun? Maybe somebody left an injection needle where I laboured to pull weeds from a downtown flowerbed.

My eye caught movement. I saw the attacker rallying other wasps to arms. I fled.

The Mouth
Nelson Agustín

The gaping hole in the earth called, The Mouth of Hell, was a popular tourist attraction. Nigel had waited for the crowd to go away before he yelled at the cavernous void in front of him. "Hello!"

His voice didn't echo back. Instead, a strange raspy one responded.

"You're next."

Guilty
Mary Long-Shimanke

"I didn't know how to be a good mother," I say to my husband. "I was distant and cold with her. We were too young to be parents. I treated Mom the same, it's true. This is a form of karma, the worst kind."

"Stop beating yourself up," he says.

In Whirls of Darkness
Kathryn Reilly

By day, a scrapper gathers discarded metal from the city's dark labyrinths.

By night, her mechanical genius unfurls as she lovingly builds a clockwork mice army. Small enough to travel anywhere, tiny gears scurry sleek-bodied mice throughout the city, gathering secrets—tipping the balance of power once and for all.

Cast Black
Kathy A. Smith

The rain stopped, but the ambulance lights were still flashing. The wind howled, tearing branches off a nearby tree. The world felt dark and empty.

Now it was.

George's childhood sweetheart lay dead in the street, his unborn baby inside.

Grief-stricken, he took out his gun and shot himself dead.

Work

Elaine Jameson

Jay entered her office, eyes empty.

"I got your email. Were you threatening me?"

Tammy went cold. She excused herself and mechanically walked to her car. Her brain faded from reality. She was not herself for a minute. She sat, blood pounding.

A shot rifled through the air. She nodded.

The Perfect Pitch
Sharon Lancaster

The room vibrated with the tenor of Pavarotti.

"Te voglio bene assaje,

Ma tanto bene sai"

(I love you very much!

So much, so much, you know)

Suddenly the sound of shattering glass interrupted my reverie.

Startled, I picked up the softball and tossed it back to the pitcher.

Liberating Death

Rania Stone

"Am I dead?" Jack blinked to clear the blood from his eyes.

"Not yet, but soon." Cherry swatted him on the head. "Your father's dead, though, and I'm leaving."

Cherry took the money and grabbed her son's hand. They ran out the door as sirens wailed.

She was finally free.

A Sigh of Welcome
Anna Cavouras

The pillow murmurs welcome, the fabric creased like an ancient map. Sometimes I hear the low hum of lingering anxiety.

Occasionally the pillow bewitches my eyelids, pulling them closed as if weighted by tiny anchors, relief washing over me in waves.

The night is not written, but the day is.

Duck 'n Gnome
Michele Rule

A rubber duck and a garden gnome joined a folk band on a cruise ship.

Duck played a great washtub bass and Gnome a mean fiddle.

One day, Gnome slipped on a banana peel, fell overboard, and sank to the bottom.

Duck sang the blues and floated on without him.

Patronized
Anne Minnings

"Is that smoke coming out of your ears?"

"OMG! She's so patronizing! She had an opinion on everything but no depth of knowledge or often even a passing acquaintance with the facts. I think my head's going to explode."

"So … not the sharpest knife in the drawer?"

"Knife? She's a spoon."

Out of the Closet
Nelson Agustín

You thought they were gone, but there's always one left behind. You slowly peer out from the closet.

The ghastly carnage lay before you, silent. You tentatively step out. You meet a pair of yellow eyes just behind the door.

Dammit, you curse. I should have stayed in the closet.

Waters Run Deep
Sharon Lancaster

"But I loved him," she drawled, inhaling slowly on the dirty cigarette butt.

Flaking nail polish told the story of ancient manicures, flowing down to knuckles thickened by malnutrition and hard work.

"I really loved him," she repeated, staring down at the swirling waters.

"That's why I let him go."

Work like a Dog
Eileen Harris

He thoroughly reviewed the family's monthly finances. Nutrition expenses, delicacies, pedicures, jewellery, baubles—it was all adding up.

Things needed to change, and fast, else he'd be chasing his tail forever.

Fido had done the math.

He would submit his formal recommendation to the family: The cat had to go.

Epic
Christy Hartman

He must keep still. A small flashlight illuminates the cave; he hopes the light's not seen outside. His evening's filled with zombie battles and princess rescues. Exhaustion burns his eyes. He persists.

Suddenly, bright light floods the cave.

His mother growls, "Tommy! Put away the book. It's time to sleep."

The Siren

Nelson Agustín

"I can't live without you," Antonio cried. "Please take me with you!"

"If you come with me, you will never see your family again." Her eyes were like iridescent pearls.

"Take me now!" he pleaded.

She bared her sharp teeth before dragging him down the murky depths of the lagoon.

The Robert Frost Murder
Marlene Lewis

Doug saw a fork in the trail as he hiked England's ancient Lindow Moss.

He veered off toward the meadow, cheerfully imitating Robert Frost's decision to take "the one less traveled by."

Almost immediately, he sank up to his waist in a bog.

As he was sucked down, he damned Frost.

Flames of Fear
Eileen Harris

She held the lit match for just a moment before tossing it onto the gas-soaked countertop.

She watched the flames rise as she backed slowly out of the room.

It may have seemed extreme to some, but it was the only way she could confidently get rid of the spider.

Drops
Kristi Clifton

Drops fall into the target eye. Drive. Check-in, day surgery. More drops. Blood pressure. Into O.R. On with the cyclops hood.

The voice says, "Follow the bright light."

What is that sawing sound? Was that a scalpel? Fight the fear. Follow the bright light.

Done.

Sit up slowly.

Technicolour restored.

The Dolls
Nelson Agustín

My eight-year-old, Lucia, had been staring at her late grandmama's antique doll collection for a long time. I heard her whispering to them.

"Sweetie," I murmured, "if you like your grandmama's dolls, we can take them home with us."

Lucia turned and glared at me.

"They demand a sacrifice, Mama."

It Started Slowly
Tess Corps

The horse came to me. He was charming and uncomplicated until that one day, he wasn't. He had bucked me off in a blind panic.

Clearly, the connection had not been completed by me as his leader.

By nature, this is what a horse wants, so together, we restarted slowly.

Plan Ahead
Eileen Harris

Jack and Jill went out for a walk. They grew thirsty and travelled to a well where Jack had a misstep.

As Jill ran to help, she also experienced a terrible fall. Jack and Jill were treated in hospital for mild concussions.

Upon returning home, they immediately ordered water bottles.

Begin Again
by Marilyn J. Brown

Inaction versus a leap of faith, a choice is made. Then you deal with it.

This time my gut hurt. In grief, I glared solidly at the scenario in my head, picked up the pen, and signed the document.

A silent tear and my forever home was mine no longer.

Sally's Song
Eileen Harris

Sally loved visiting Mr. Mack Donald's farm and learning the names of the animals.

The nearby road was frequented by ambulances. The sound of blaring sirens always surprised Sally's mother, and she would exclaim "Oh!" each time.

Now Sally sings the names of Mr. Donald's animals with an "E-I-E-I Oh!"

The Man in Black
Nelson Agustín

"So this is it, then?" I asked the Man in Black. "No judgement, no afterlife?"

He shrugged. "I don't know what to say to you. I'm just doing my job."

He swung his gleaming scythe and snagged my neck. Soon I was trailing behind him like a wisp of smoke.

The Man
Elaine Jameson

"I'm tellin' ya. There's a battle to fight. The time is nigh. We won't back down!" The man in the green cap gesticulated wildly.

"Our war. Our triumph!"

Ping! The elevator doors opened. Astonished employees hurried into the lobby for lunch.

They left the odd man, arms raised, alone.

Imposter Syndrome
Jennifer Platts-Fanning

"The fragility of human existence will always be warmed by the sun," she mused. "However, tonight, you'll join me under the weeping moon."

"Am I pretty enough to be a vampire?" he asked. Rain streaked down the sharp cheekbone, brow furrowed, contemplating his Japanese death poem.

His vulnerability, her aphrodisiac.

The Ceremony
Nelson Agustín

He knew he must keep very still. The infernal chanting had stopped, but the unholy screeching went on.

He pushed himself up slowly into a sitting position and peeked through the bushes.

A gaping void circled with endless rings of sharp filthy teeth screeched at him on the other side.

The Attack
Elaine Jameson

Perfect camouflage, and in just a few steps, a perfect sightline.

Another is drawn to the commotion, armed with bone-crushing intention. The opportunist creeps forward. Others lurk, hoping to benefit from the fallout.

The attack happens swiftly. Suddenly, the target disappears.

Defeated, she would have to await the next sale.

Drabbles: 100 Word Stories

The Importance of Charitable Support
Eileen Harris

Since her husband died, tending the garden had become Charity's daily occupation. She carefully removed the weeds from around her collection of Amorphophallus titanum. A flower better known as the corpse flower. It was renowned for its rotting stench and its endangered status.

Charity dutifully maintained the flower for the city's annual Floral Fair, which helped her educate the community about this rare organism.

She meticulously tended to it so that the community would guarantee its beauty would remain protected for future decades.

It would also ensure that the husband she murdered could never be dug up from under it.

Princess

By Kathryn Reilly

Her shocked, silent kingdom watches as the bloodied princess raises a crimson-splattered sword. In her right hand, the monster's severed head hangs, proof of her prowess, which she throws at her father's feet.

"I saved myself, and indeed, all of you; therefore, I demand the right to choose whom I marry."

Silence stretches as the king understands the gravity of this request—finally, he nods.

A radiant smile brightens the princess's face before she proclaims, "I choose myself. I will love, honor, and obey myself always until death parts me from this world, delivering me to the next great adventure."

Shhh
Kelly Pawlik

He knew to keep very still. Footsteps moved down the hall toward him. He sucked in his breath, hoping he was hidden by the shadow of the plush couch.

The figure moved into the room carrying an oversized bag. They paused. He wondered if they knew he was there.

The figure moved to the tree, which was illuminated with tiny white lights. Slowly, they reached into the bag and removed several boxes, placing each one gingerly around the tree.

He took a small breath. The figure turned and padded out of the room.

He'd discovered the true magic behind Christmas.

Breaking News!
Mary Long-Shimanke

"Again, our top story is the newest Supreme Court decision. A solid affirmative vote of six to three on the latest decision in a string of reproductive cases that have been put before the court in previous months.

"It follows the recent decisions on abortion and the ban of all contraceptives, including prophylactics, gels, birth control pills, and IUDs.

"The 22-1790 affirmative ruling confirms sperm is now considered the true beginning of human life. Vasectomies are banned and considered a criminal offence in the entire United States.

"And now back to you, John, for the final word on the weather."

The Boy Who Lived in the Forest
Sally Quon

I picture him—long, toffee-coloured hair and azure-tinted glasses—like John Lennon used to wear. He lived alone, squatting on crown land, in a shack built with deadfall and cedar boughs.

I longed to see it, gather wood for the fire, and make love on a bed of moss.

He was the free spirit I could have been if life handed me a different kind of fruit.

I don't remember his name, only that he would bring me a fistful of wildflowers and grasses he gathered as he walked from forest to beach. I'd give him a pint of Guinness.

Go, Go, Stop!
P. F. Brown

Go, go, go … Stop! She appeared suspended on the brink.

Four young girls were experimenting with boundaries and trust. The three older kids were rolling down the hill to the pond edge, the youngest navigating. She was getting bored.

And so, when her sisters suggested she take a turn rolling, she was willing to trade her reticence for a bit of daring.

Go, go, go …

No! Could she trust them?

It felt reckless. The hill was too long.

SPLASH!

Spluttering, flailing, raging, sinking.

Bigger girls crying at the pond edge.

Slam. Leap, leap, grab.

Rescued from oblivion.

Thank you, Mommy.

A Good Impression
Stevi Stephens

Barry was determined to impress his fiancée's parents. Samantha's folks had treated them to dinner at an exclusive restaurant.

All went well until Barry made a trip to the gents room. When he returned, Samantha nudged him and whispered, "xyz!"

Without looking, Barry reached into his lap and zipped up his fly. The evening meal ended pleasantly after coffee and conversation. Barry leaped to his feet to help Samantha with her chair.

As he moved, so did all of the dishes on the table. The crescendo of crashing crockery had everyone's focused attention on the tablecloth zipped into Barry's fly.

Space Delicacies
Kathryn Reilly

Approaching the listing vessel, Intrepidus's salvage crew sought fuel, food, and coveted black market goods. Boarding quickly, they found their assigned areas.

"Check in."

"Somara. Three months of food, including a greens rotator. Transporting in ten."

"Melur. Medical stocked. Transporting now."

"Haba. Fuel available. Transporting in fifteen."

"Reggie. Quarters are gold mines with weapons. Transporting in twenty."

"Thenin. Trashed lab. My God, the bodies. They're in pieces. They're mov—"

It was quite a successful salvage of the Intrepidus's crew.

Zaverns dined, delighting in the human-unique proteins tantalizing their tongues.

They'd always been thankful this particular species mastered space travel.

Services Rendered
Angela Rebrec

"Honestly." She apologized again. "I forgot my wallet at home."

If she had looked closely, and if the streetlights had been brighter, she would have seen Dimitri smirk. "Valet parking is fifteen dollars—you owe for services rendered."

Annoyed with how many rich-bitches had scammed him lately, he reasoned they deserved some payback. "Here's the deal—lick my boot, and you can go."

She inspected his footwear. "Are those real Doc Martins? Or knockoffs?"

"They're real."

If he had looked closely and the streetlights had been brighter, Dimitri would have seen the woman smirk right before she tasted his boot.

Commercial Jingles Of a Certain Vintage
Kathy Robinson

"Captain. Crunch the numbers now."

"Ask Sanders to use the quicker picker-upper on his chicken fingers."

"The colonel who takes a licking and keeps on ticking? Ask him, 'Where's the beef?' and it'll be mm, mm good."

"If his fingers do the walking through these yellow pages, my work is ruined."

"It might be the best a man can get."

"Have it your way, but it absolutely, positively needs to get there overnight. Give him something that melts in your mouth, not your hand."

"Cross my heart. Go deliver your Hawaiian punch."

"It'll be magically delicious. "

Two all-beef patties … "

The Ache
Kristi Clifton

I would have followed you to the ends of the earth, but your invitation was issued a bit late.

I ached when your letter arrived just as my honeymoon ended.

But I gave over to the current I jumped into and was swept through the years. And they were mostly good, those years.

But sometimes, it got quiet, and the ache would return. And the possibilities would play in my mind. I always thought there was still time.

Now this, your obituary, stumbled upon late one night. An abrupt end to the possibilities.

But not the end of the ache.

A Night's Endeavour
Kathy A. Smith

Donna poured whiskey into her teacup while Doug sharpened the saw.

"Let's wait until midnight this time," he said in a deep, gravelly voice.

Donna nodded, finished her drink, then went to the barn and saddled the horses.

They headed out, with their handy dandy sack of tools and shovels roped onto their steeds.

Arriving at their destination, they dismounted and grabbed their shovels and a large box they had towed in a little cart.

Fog shrouded the moon as they entered the gloomy church graveyard.

Stopping to dig at each burial plot, they placed small bouquets of fresh flowers.

Beneath the Surface
Anna Cavouras

Once while rafting, our boat flipped before anyone knew it would. It was a calm day on the river, until it wasn't. I was launched deep underwater.

Disoriented, I contemplated which way was up for a small eternity. Then I saw my own bubbles: tiny aquatic breadcrumbs leading me to the surface.

I came up underneath the overturned boat for a breath. The river roared after the silence beneath.

Panic seeped in as I clutched the rope attached to the boat.

I forced myself underwater again, to the other side, into the sun and the calm part of the river.

My Beloved, Humanity's Bane
Hazel Ragaire

Prior to our planet's implosion, we relocated beloved creatures where they could survive. I protect the Brosno dragon.

A carnivore, like Earth's Spinosaurus, ample perch and burbot sustain her, but she craves sapiens. Her first human flesh belonged to Vikings ruling the Kievan Rus' state; their fierceness flavored the flesh.

Batu Khan lost many Golden Horde warriors to razor-sharp maws. She altered history's course: terrified troops fled, saving Novgorod from the Tatar-Mongol invasion.

WWII celebrated her consumption of a German plane. She didn't eat the plane, though its German pilots were tasty.

Today's menu features hikers—all curious travelers welcome.

Lost
Christy Hartman

The night is cold and lonely, surrounded by concrete walls. I close my eyes and try to remember how it felt to run with Beau in the grass behind our house.

Our warm bed by the fire, family movie nights curled together on the couch, picnics, and Frisbee in the park, are all distant memories.

I hear Beau's soft cries. I can't comfort him.

Daylight brings warmth and hope.

The sound of footsteps makes me rise. A little girl stops in front of my cage and crouches down. I wag my tail and hope she says I'm a good boy.

Of Love and Legacies
Kathryn Reilly

She propositions the dragon: "I return with your head and change women's and dragons' futures."

Mother dragon considers.

"I've sung many dragons to life beyond. Noble death prevents future death. You'll save dragons from man?"

"Yes. I submit."

The princess strokes her scales, singing of hope.

When dragon mother dreams, the princess severs her head.

***

Brandishing the head, she demands a warrior's rights before the kingdom. The king agrees. She inherits everything, recalibrating the world.

She ascends as queen, first of her name. She trains female warriors who ride, honour and protect dragons.

New mothers rise, reshaping the world.

The Tyrant
Eileen Harris

I carefully stirred the peas and carrots, removing any peas that had lost their skin or become misshapen. Then I checked on the chicken to ensure it was cooked but not too dry.

I flinched when I heard a noise, but it was just the meat sizzling in the pan. Cooking for the tyrant had become my job, but I still couldn't adjust to it.

It was my choice, I reminded myself. I cautiously served him dinner. It did not go well. He hurled it to the floor and began screaming at me.

I shirked, clutching my wine. Blasted toddlers.

Skip the Carnage
Angela Rebrec

"Curse these blasted directions!" Frankle bellowed as he swerved his wagon around another bloated toadstool. He knew there'd be no tip if the food arrived cold.

Paper bags and boxes rustle in the back as he steered his giant badger left, then right, then left again through the dense thicket.

Nearing a turbulent river, the wagon's jacklight illuminated a troll posing menacingly. "Who dares cross this bridge!" he roared.

"Your delivery's here."

Frankle waited for payment. The troll dug through the bags, counted the takeout boxes, and removed one.

He opened the lid, sniffed, and sneered. "These pixies are cold."

The Winner
Anne Minnings

Ready. Set. Go!

Gerod lunged forward at a slight angle, managing to throw his nearest rival, Carl, off balance.

"This is it," he thought as he surged ahead. There were ten contestants running, and proving himself the fastest of them all was Gerod's burning ambition.

Gerod's arms pumped. Fifty yards, halfway there. Breathing hard, he crossed the finish line seconds later.

A moment passed before he realized there was silence. No noise? Where were the cheers, whistles, and applause? Gerod spun around.

The rest of the contestants were clustered around Carl.

Gerod proved himself best in a field of one.

Doing Bach
Nat Kischuck

The pharmacist peers over her glasses. "This is quite a dose of Bach. What are you taking it for?"

"Prelude Number 1."

"C major?"

You nod. Fingertips burning.

"This much Bach enzyme might block your catalysis of other composers." Frowning—judgy. "Are you doing the whole Well-Tempered Clavier?"

How can you explain what you are? Your implacable left-handed heart. Your reverberant right-handed brain. Your revulsion for any other enzymes in your body.

What if she won't fill it? Fingertips blistering.

She peers again, sighs. "I did some Chopin once, didn't agree with me either. Okay, Mr. Gould, here you go."

In the Widow's Garden
Christy Hartman

My hairdresser's matchmaking again. Her electrician this time.

I go on dates, knowing you and I will ramble barefoot through the garden afterward, our footprints visible in the damp grass. We dissect the latest fish in the shallow pool of eligible men. We laugh about skinny jeans, well-done steaks, and pinky rings.

In our final month together, you told me to search for love again. Magical love, like ours.

This evening, the electrician took me to the fair. Lemonade. A rollercoaster.

I run to the garden when I return. Flushed, eager to talk.

Silence.

Tonight, the only footprints are mine.

Overkill
Stevi Stephens

During the Depression, the Everglades Research Project requisitioned a gator gun. The FBI supplied a sawed-off shotgun. When a water moccasin dropped into the airboat, it was blasted with both barrels.

Both the snake and the boat bottom disintegrated. Two miserable scientists slogged back to land.

A government form was required to explain the loss of the boat. An office clerk had a brilliant idea.

"We have lots of unaccounted losses, so I'll list all of them in the boat contents."

That form eventually returned to the office stamped APPROVED.

A hand-written comment noted, "It's no damned wonder it sank."

The Dawn
Corina Hartley

Phantom pain comes to haunt me, embodies my brain, liver, and soul.

Visions bold and bright, soothed only by this coal.

Animated afore me, constant reel of past,

Turn off the television. That's my mind, spinning fast.

Partake of this, drink of that. Inhale once more. Stop the chat.

Heavy heart, sandy mouth, trails of truth, repeat.

Continue with this journey, my maker. I'll meet

Heavy burden, I'm so tired, laden, weighed down.

Goodbye, to this world, I've come to get my crown.

Alas, the dawn is here—the day will start anew.

Sun has surely awakened. Nightmares bid adieu.

Nowhere to Hide
Eileen Harris

I'm hiding in a dark, locked room. My body tenses as I hear his footsteps coming. He's looking for me.

I piddle a little and hope he can't hear me exhale. His footsteps stop at the door. The knob twists slowly but resists against the lock. Another jiggle of the knob, and he gives up, but I hear a thump.

He's still there. A few fingers begin to curl up from under the door.

I panic. He's found me. How did he find me? I was silent. I was quick.

He shrieks, "Mommy, stop peeing! I need a yogurt now!"

Germs
Stevi Stephens

Pam suffered from germaphobia. Her animal-loving son suffered more. Pam wouldn't even allow a pet goldfish.

Levi begged until Pam agreed to visit a dude ranch. There were conditions. Pam wouldn't go near the animals and must inspect the kitchen.

The kitchen passed inspection. The cook assured Pam that the dishes were as clean as hot water and soap could get them.

Pam read on the veranda and watched her son ride horses and play with dogs.

Driving from the ranch, Pam praised the dogs. Levi agreed but mentioned their strange names. "What were their names?"

"Hot, Water, and Soap."

Maggie's Map
Tess Corps

Maggie, at fifty-two years young and far too slim, has the lines on her face that show the story of her life.

Having juggled a full-time career of training horses, difficult relationships, and always pleasing others, she's lived a lifetime at full throttle. So much so that she has missed out on what she really needed. She has a radiant smile that she easily shares with all she encounters. Behind it lies a private existence of insecurities and loneliness.

Maggie now knows what she needs and, with new determination, will seek to find it, removing the walls that encased her.

Kidnapped
Darcy Nybo

Helen walked down the poorly maintained forest service road.

The muffled voice on the phone had told her that if she wanted to see her boyfriend again, she was to take the first path to her right, find a clearing with a red chair, sit in it, and blindfold herself. She did as she was told.

"Hello?" she called out.

Silence.

There was a snuffling sound. Something warm and wet touched her cheek.

Helen ripped off the blindfold to find a puppy on her lap.

Around its neck was a beautiful ring and a small note that said, "Marry me."

Battle at Sunrise
Christy Hartman

"Five is too high!" Tom raced over and turned down the silver dial, narrowly averting disaster.

"Well, three is not going to do the job. You're insane." Sue pushed his hand away and rotated the dial to the right.

"You're going to ruin everything. This is my choice, and I say five is too high."

Their fingers clash on the shiny surface, the battle for control becomes more and more heated.

Tom feels a sharp elbow jab into his side. He turns the dial all the way to the left.

Pop!

They stare silently at the perfect piece of toast.

Together, Not Forever
Marilyn J. Brown

The weathered log near the bank provided a suitable resting spot. The aged woman stared blankly towards the pond, drifting across decades of memories, adventures, and grief.

A breeze stirred her blouse just enough to tell her evening was approaching. She should be heading back. Soon, but not at that moment.

She reached into her shoulder bag for her pill bottle. Two ought to do, followed up with a generous swig from the bottle also tucked in the bag.

"Honey, I'll be there soon," she said as she closed her eyes.

It was a tough walk back to the house.

Sleep Tight
Theresa Leinemann

My childhood summers smelled of campfire smoke and burnt marshmallows. We slept in a basic tent trailer, two kids to a side.

Mom and Dad got the camper. I made my little brother sleep on the outer edge. After a windstorm sent the canvas roof sailing across the campground last year, Mom sewed a new one, held in place by elastic at the corners.

At dawn, the door zipper woke me up. A small hand pushed a sleeping bag and pillow through the opening.

My brother crawled in, twigs in his hair, and grinned. "I fell out of bed again."

Finding Dudley
Tess Corps

Eva had lost her beloved little dog after exploring the world together. When Daizee abruptly died, she had been heartbroken.

A year later, while scrolling on Facebook, Dudley penetrated her heart. The quirky dog pictured called out to her.

Looking into his eyes, Eva's heart filled again. Dudley was in a shelter in Houston, Texas, and he desperately needed a home.

The van arrived on that cold and rainy night. Dudley tentatively came out, and Eva was handed the leash.

Dropping to her knees, Dudley laid his exhausted head on her shoulder. Eva embraced him, whispering, "I got you, buddy."

Fortune Cookie
Marlene Lewis

As he drove home from PeKing Restaurant, Arthur scoffed at the idiocy of reading the generic statements in fortune cookies. Those things were mass produced in a Chinese cookie factory!

Yet, he was compelled to read them for some unfathomable reason. There was something unfinished, unsatisfactory about leaving a fortune cookie in its cellophane wrapper, unopened, hiding its foolish fortune.

Arthur shook his head to clear his mind of these ramblings.

He missed the stop sign. The crash was horrific, with fatalities in both vehicles.

Investigators overlooked the tiny slip of paper on the seat of Arthur's car: "Luck abounds."

First Wife
Christy Hartman

From the front pew, Sarah watched the young bride's hands shake as she walked.

Fifteen years ago, Sarah walked the same aisle towards the same groom. He had been old that spring morning. Today he was ancient.

Six brides added to her house since that first wedding. She wouldn't allow another.

Last year Sarah gathered her strength to flee, selling her wedding dress for a bus ticket west. His violent hands caught her before she boarded. Today's escape would be permanent.

Her hand slid into her pocket and touched cold metal. With one practiced motion, Sarah stood, aimed, and fired.

Sue
Sally Quon

The full moon hangs low in the sky tonight, so close I imagine touching it.

The scent of leaves about to turn clings to my nostrils. The northern lights dance in the sky, ribbons of green that shift and flow against a backdrop of stars.

I think about Sue. She's a fifty-three-year-old, ninety-seven-pound, cancer-ridden crack addict who lives in a park on the riverbank.

I wonder, does she see the lights in the sky tonight? Do they make her believe in a higher power?

And then I thank the gods for another week of warm weather, especially for Sue's sake.

Photograph
Maggie Jackson

"Mommy, why do I only have one grandma and no brothers or sisters?" four-year-old Tanner asked.

"I'll be right back," she said. "I have something to show you."

Tanner's mom returned with two pictures. "This one is your Grandma Deb. She died about ten years ago."

Tanner examined the photo.

"And this one is of your big sister, Sophia. She got sick and died about a year before you were born."

"Oh, Mommy, don't be silly," he said as he pointed to the photos. "That's me when I was Debbie, and the other one is me when I was Sophia!"

The Lottery Winner

Anne Minnings

Dear John,

I received your formal letter, so I am responding in kind.

Yes, I'm enjoying my lottery winnings. Several millions does much to take the sting out of a breakup.

No, I won't be sharing it with you, although I did get a chuckle out of your suggestion that we split it fifty-fifty.

I laughed aloud at your threat to call a lawyer.

Go ahead, but don't spend too much as I have date-stamped proof that the ticket was purchased after you left.

So thoughtful of you to dump me by email.

Yours, with a touch of schadenfreude,

Julie

White Linen Lady
Corina Hartley

She glides by, dressed in white linen and a false smile. Twice.

Intentional with her destination yet turned around by Murphy's Law. Her skin aged, gently rouged, and perfumed, silver hair coifed to perfection. She catches my eye as I admire her confident gait, hiding well a repeatedly practiced quandary.

I pick up the crystal goblet from the restaurant table and raise the aged cabernet sauvignon to my lips.

The tension she attempted to mask was palpable. I tip my head towards her with respect to her lost plight.

After all, the ladies' rooms in this establishment do fill quickly.

Mary's Coffee
Darcy Nybo

Mary poured a fresh brew of coffee and yew leaves into a go-cup and added the right amount of cream and sugar. She tightened the lid as her fifth husband entered the kitchen. Mary smiled.

She'd married all five husbands when they were sixty-three. They were sixty-five when they died. Young enough to be fun—old enough to be felled by a heart attack.

"Here you go," she said and gave him the cup. "Have a great birthday golfing with the boys."

As he left, coffee in hand, she opened Match on her computer to search for husband number six.

No More
Sue Boghean

Sally trembled, and her breathing became shallow as she clumsily hung up the phone.

"No more," she whispered.

Sally instantly calmed as her eyes went from the sharpened butcher knife to the gun cabinet to her small canister of poison, hidden in plain sight.

Sally believed that orchestrating multiple murder plans was the only thing that kept her sane.

That evening Sally jumped into the truck when Mason pulled up. She took a chug of his beer. She was instantly dizzy.

Mason drove up to the grave Sally had dug in the farm's back field last full moon.

"What? No!"

Postcards: 240-250 Word Stories

The Lake
Sally Quon

As the water closed over my head, panic bubbled in my chest. How did this happen? My internal voice was mocking me, telling me how ridiculous I was for getting into this situation, telling me I was an idiot who didn't deserve to live. Darwin's Law and all.

I tried reasoning with myself, partly to fight the voices and partly to keep the panic from bursting out of me like the alien in that movie. There was no reasoning with me. Part of me wanted to give in to the chaos.

If I could stay calm, I could make my way to shore, but the wrong parts were trying to float, keeping my head from reaching the surface. After everything I had been through in my life, was this how I would die? It was Ironic.

I was never afraid of water. I was always in control. It turns out that was an illusion, shattered by one windy day, one rogue wave. With a final, desperate push, my feet went down, and my head came up. Hands reached for me from the floating dock, pulled me up, and laid me on sun-warmed wood. Eyes closed, I tried to regain control of my body, thrashing heartbeat, spattered breath.

I didn't see my rescuers. When I opened my eyes, I was alone.

Maybe they weren't even real. Maybe it was Naitaka, the spirit of the lake, the one white settlers called Ogopogo.

Strange Brew
Ann Tiplady

On Friday, Hazel and I met for coffee and lunch. When Hazel had her coffee, we settled outside, where it was warmer. I went back in for a sandwich.

The sign said they could make gluten-free sandwiches. I said I'd like one. The young woman behind the counter looked at me helpfully, so I asked for a menu.

There was no menu, she said, the options were in the glass case, meaning the ready-to-buy regular sandwiches on display. The first was ham and cheese. I said that sounded fine.

She looked at me expectantly. "Do you want lettuce in that?"

"Oh, is that a choice? Yes, please."

Then she explained that their lettuce was spinach. They don't have lettuce; they have spinach. But they call it lettuce. Do I want the lettuce, seeing as it's spinach? I generally avoid spinach, as I don't like the oxalic acid feeling in my mouth.

"No thanks on the spinach-lettuce."

Thinking to bypass further discussion along this line, I switched to the chicken and pesto sandwich.

She explained that their pesto is tapenade, but for gluten-free sandwiches, they substitute mayonnaise for the tapenade. Is that okay?

Sure, I said, thinking, *You call it pesto, but it's actually tapenade, you call it lettuce, but it's actually spinach. What thought process came up with this?*

I wondered how much time was wasted with all these explanations. But it wouldn't work to just start by asking, "Would you like spinach in that?" because that would be weird.

The Funeral
Mary Long-Shimanke

"You know, when Mom found herself pregnant with you, they tried to find a doctor who would perform an abortion. But it was the fifties.

My brother's face told me he had no idea.

"By the time she had me, she was suicidal."

"If that's true, then why the hell would she have more children?"

I leaned in. "You know, you don't always have a choice as a woman. Sometimes it's not your choice what happens in your bed at night."

The words hung between us like on a clothesline. Nasty words pinned up for the entire world to see.

"That probably explains why she beat me," he said.

"She didn't beat you. You made that up to shock us. You're lying. Everyone knew that, even him."

I looked down at our father in his casket.

"I don't know why you defended him. You were betting on the wrong horse, even you knew it, but you couldn't admit it," I said.

"I think you're just trying to mess with me."

"Sure, it's all a joke, sorry."

"You're such a fucking bitch. You've always been

one. All your life. Just like your mother."

"Here we go, chip off the old block."

I left then, him standing there as if surrounded by garbage, cemented against his legs. Outside, I twirled like I was five again, all the dusty memories flying off me like DNA in a centrifuge.

Walking away, I felt forty years lighter.

New Traditions
Kara Seabrook

Dad loved birds and knew them well—each call and colouring. I could tell you about the common birds like a chickadee, goldfinch, or blue jay, but the trickier ones not so much.

Thus, Bird Bingo was born. The game only applied to migratory birds returning in the spring. In order for the bird to count, you had to actually see the bird, not just hear it. Whoever saw the most birds won.

It was the second annual year, and Dad went all out and made official tracking cards to put on the fridge. That was back in March.

Now it was May, and the race was tight. There were only four birds left: the oriole, the red throated hummingbird, the eastern kingbirds, and the wood thrush. My chances of winning were slim, but I was desperate to redeem myself from getting creamed last year.

Dad had heard the oriole around our property for over a week and was on the lookout.

That's when it happened. Dad and I had just gotten home from work. I'd stopped by the kitchen table when I saw it. A male oriole flew in and perched on top of where we hang the feeders.

Before I had time to think, I heard my voice yell, "Oriole, oriole, oriole!" I couldn't believe it. One bird left to secure my spot in a tie. I was feeling confident when I saw a hummingbird the next day.

That's when we started finding them dead under the feeder.

Tale of a Mason Jar
Elaine Gugin Maddex

The Mason jar sat clean and empty at the back of the dark cubby. It patiently waited for its next assignment with great regard and anticipation.

The Mason jar never knew what treasure it would be called upon to store and protect but was always anxious to fulfill a new mission.

As it waited, it reminisced about its past contents. When the Mason jar was first purchased, it was to house Maeve's prized dill pickles. A colourful cloth was neatly tethered around the lid, and the preserves within won a blue ribbon at the county fair. A very proud moment for a Mason jar, to be sure.

Later that fall, it was filled with delicious raspberry jam, which lasted in the fridge until Christmas.

After the jar received a good scrubbing, Maeve decided to do some crafting and created a lovely display of Christmas bobbles and lights tucked inside it. The Mason jar thoroughly enjoyed looking so festive and shone with delight.

The cubby door opened, and Maeve reached in. The Mason jar immediately swelled with excitement. Is this it? Is it me she's searching for? Yes!

Maeve carried the Mason jar over to the counter and gave it a quick wipe before setting it down. She opened the lid, picked up a large plastic bag of sewing buttons, and poured them in. The merry sound of clinking buttons thrilled the Mason jar. It was quite satisfied in knowing this was its newfound purpose.

Definitely Not Haunted
Kelly Pawlik

Arthur pulled into the driveway, admiring the bungalow. He saw it in all its glory: fragrant red rose bushes, a flawless lawn, a freshly painted exterior. But he knew what other people saw.

He opened the door and shifted his feet onto the pavement. Arthur held onto the door as he pulled himself from his LeSabre. His body creaked.

Arthur closed the door, moved to the passenger side, and opened Ruth's door. He breathed in the smell of rosewood, bergamot, and a pleasant combination of fruity notes. He sighed, content at the familiar smell of her perfume.

A teenage boy mowed a lawn down the road. He'd mowed several properties since Arthur had gone out. Everyone seemed to outsource these days.

"Home again, home again," Arthur murmured. He removed the sign from the front seat, smiling at the memory of Ruth tending their rose bushes while he kneeled on the grass, removing each weed from the lawn by hand.

A home to be proud of.

He'd come to terms with being unable to manage

the lawn, but Ruth didn't like being reminded the roses were beyond her.

Arthur closed the passenger door and made his way up the drive. Ruth's perfume trailed behind him. Arthur hammered the sign into the garden.

It wasn't enough.

Perhaps if the boy did some of the yard work, but Ruth didn't want anyone touching her roses. Arthur felt her disdain.

"Maybe tomorrow," he murmured, going inside. "Rest your soul, my love."

From the Highway, the River Looks like a Grand Slam Breakfast for Dinner
Angela Rebrec

"Listen—I don't need anyone to make sure I get there," Joelle growled as she geared down from thirteen to nine, the highway's grade ever steepening. "It's creepy you're following me with your macho man-truck."

Matt's hazards flashed as he drove at a crawl beside a pedaling Joelle, the river narrowing in the canyon below the shoulder's height. "I just don't feel right leaving you with no spare tire and town twenty kilometres away."

Matt missed Joelle's eye roll as she kept her sight on the asphalt.

He provided his driver's license, hoping it would make the situation less weird, while simultaneously trying to convince her to put her bike in the cargo bed and drive her to town as she struggled with the inner tube and pump.

"I planned this solo road trip knowing there'd be flat tires," she said, wiping sweat off her forehead with the back of her hand. "I don't need rescuing—especially by some creepo like you."

Matt smiled at the smeared chain grease she left

behind on her forehead.

"What's your problem?" Joelle wondered out loud.

"There's grease on your forehead."

Joelle looked down at her hands.

"Hey!" Matt yelled through the open passenger-side window as another car honked, passing them on the left. "I know you must think I'm some mass murderer or something, but, can I buy you dinner when we get into town?"

Joelle pedaled harder. "If you're stupid enough to follow me all the way to Yale, then why not."

Bird Strike
Ann Tiplady

A short wintery day was ending when I heard a crack sound on in the big living room window. A bird had struck the glass.

Fearing the worst, I hurried out and found a small sparrow lying in the garden below the window. Dazed, its head swiveled around as though it were drunk. At least it was alive.

It couldn't fly, though. If I left it there, Cleo, the next-door cat, the huntress who owns our garden, might find it. I'd encountered her once, early on a lovely spring morning, crunching on a small bird, perhaps a spring migrant who now would never raise babies.

I didn't dare leave the bird for Cleo to find. And it was getting dark and cold, both conditions working against recovery.

With gloves on, I gently lifted it into a box and folded the flaps closed. They weigh so little, little birds like this. They almost feel like nothing in the hand.

On the floor, just inside the front door, with a large book on top to keep it closed, the box was silent. Inside, in the quiet blackness, the bird could either recover or quietly die.

Early next morning, the sun was just rising, and scratching sounds were coming from the box. Outside, I opened the box and peeked. A bright-eyed, alert sparrow burst from the box and was gone across the garden.

We've changed the windows since then. We have few bird strikes now.

Karen and Carl
Kathy A. Smith

Karen screamed as loudly as she could.
Carl playfully threatened her with a knife as he backed her into their bedroom, undressing her with his eyes.

It was the kind of made-up fight that left her super aroused.

Can we really pull this crazy thing off? she wondered.

She screamed again as Carl slammed the door and locked it. Yelling obscenities, he smashed a bottle of whiskey on the table and threw dishes at the wall.

The ruckus could be heard loud and clear for miles on the hot summer day.

Inside the bedroom, Karen fought mounting panic and felt parched from the midday heat and their fiery exchange. But she was thrilled to be part of Carl's bad boy ways. Almost casually, she moved to the closet to retrieve a hidden pistol. It was locked and loaded. She caressed it as if it were a delicate child.

Suddenly, she heard another voice.

"Gotta call about a disturbance here. What's goin' on?"

"Nuttin'," Carl muttered. "Nuttin' at all."

Karen heard heavy boots coming her way. The doorknob rattled but would not budge.

The voice yelled, "Stand back!" then kicked the door in.

Perfectly positioned, Karen aimed squarely at the target, just as she had practiced. A single shot rang out.

Within seconds, the young county officer slumped down dead on the floor.

"Good one, babe," Carl laughed. "Quick, grab his gun and keys, and let's get outta this godforsaken town."

"Happily," Karen cooed. "Where they'll never find us."

Deadlines
Marlene Lewis

"What are you going to do with the body?"

"I don't know yet."

"You don't have much time, you know."

"I do know, and that's why I'm getting nervous."

"Why can't you weigh it down with chains and dump it in the middle of the lake?"

"It's a koi pond and only seven feet deep in the middle."

"I don't suppose you want to just leave it there until someone finds it?"

"No, that gets complicated."

"Do you want another drink?"

"Of course, I do! Same thing. No, make it a double this time."

"Okay, but you need to keep your wits about you until this is settled."

"That's why I asked you to meet me here. You've done this before. I hoped you'd give me an idea or two."

"Hey, you think I wrote *101 Ways to Get Rid of a Body for Dummies*? My own method may not be creative, but it always works. No stress."

"You do the same thing every time you kill someone?"

"Sure. Just push him off something high depending on where he's killed. Edge of the Grand Canyon, penthouse window, grain silo, cruise ship. My favorite was off the helipad on the roof of St. Joe's hospital. A gift for the pre-med students."

"The body's in the first-floor bedroom."

"Bummer."

"Oh, hello, Officer. Do you want to speak with us? What? The twit in the next booth called you? Good Lord, no! We're mystery writers, and I'm under deadline to my editor!"

Moment with a Stranger
Fern G. Z. Carr

I jumped up and down when I heard the news! My sister had decided to move to Kelowna—her dream for the past thirty years.

Both of us scrambled to make all sorts of plans while my mind raced as to how I could do everything possible to streamline her transition.

One of our strategies was to arrange for my sister to view apartments via FaceTime. She was enthusiastic about one suite in particular, so she contacted the property manager and made an appointment for me to be her iPhone cinematographer. I was delighted to oblige.

Since I wanted to make the best impression possible on the day of the viewing, I dressed in my finest and set out to meet the manager. With a huge smile, I jaunted from the parking lot to the front entrance, where I happened to encounter a woman walking her dog. I dropped to my knee to pat the sweet little West Highland Terrier—a West Highland Terrier almost identical to my sweet little Caitlin, who had since passed away.

With a tear in my eye, I looked upward at this

woman and told her about my dog. In that instant, tears welled up in her eyes, too. She shared the story of her other Westie, who had also recently passed away.

I was struck by the intensity of our fleeting interaction thanks to our common yet unexpected bond. How overwhelming to have such a poignant moment with a stranger.

Leaving the Library in the Rain
Anna Cavouras

Standing in the library's foyer with a stack of books clutched to my chest, I wonder how I can get home.

Rain falls torrentially, filling the streets so quickly that it appears water is emerging from the sidewalk itself. A warm day and the water falls with urgency, soaking to the marrow. I feel urgency, too. It's my first Ontario summer, and the weather patterns of this unfamiliar geography are still a mystery. I wait, watching others do the same.

When I sense the rain has lightened the tiniest bit, I shove the books under my shirt wrapped in layers of free news, and dash out, convinced I can make the seven blocks to home.

At block two, the water is so deep and swift that I feel my flip-flops hover. Debris clogs my toes, and I flinch when a rat floats by. Briefly, I lose my footing. A flip-flop gets loose and threatens to ride the rapids down the hill to Lake Ontario. I snatch it and shove it back on my foot, clutching my toes tightly against the wavy plastic.

Bursting through my front door, I smile, exhilarated by the adventure. I take off my clothes and drip dry. The books have survived. I peel disintegrating news pages from their title pages.

I feel clean and bright until I look down. My feet are filthy, stained with streaks of mud. I find brightly coloured plastic wedged between my toes.

Schoolyard Bricks and Mortar
Elaine Jameson

Bonnie watches three girls twirl around in long skirts. They whip about like a twister, laughing and falling down. When boys come along, they control their twirling, so skirts don't go too high.

Bonnie wrote in her notebook. Except Ira; she don't care. Her knees is always dirty,

Once the coast is clear, Bonnie jumps from the tree, making her getaway. It's time to report back.

"Three stooges twirling again. Ira's knees are repulsive. That's the report."

"Good work, B." Henry nodded.

"Good work, B." Douglas copied, ignoring Henry's glance.

"Now to Big Tree for a spy meeting!" Henry whispered loudly.

The spies ran to the best tree in the schoolyard. They climb high into the clouds, and Bonnie pretends all the kids below are ants.

Two larger bug figures emerged with coffee mugs.

"I can't believe it. I thought all explosives were discarded long ago after Vernon stopped being a military training ground. How could this have happened?" Mr. Andrews shakes his head in disbelief.

"How do we tell the kids?" Miss Barber stood deathly still, pale, stricken.

"We certainly can't say Simon was blown up by an old WWI mortar that he and Ben were tossing back and forth on the commonage. We will need to be careful with our words."

They walk back towards the school.

The spies inch down the tree. Bonnie thinks of Simon at the desk behind her.

"What's a mortar?" she asks.

Henry looks nauseated.

Douglas scratches his eczema like always.

The Presents
Anne Minnings

"What did you bring us? What did you bring us?" The twins hopped up and down as they greeted Auntie Sally.

Sally smiled at her nieces and handed each a small box.

"Oh, is that all?" Disappointment showed in the girls' faces. They shrugged in unison and ran off to play.

The greeting was similar on Sally's next visit.

"What did you bring us? What did you bring us?" The twins hopped up and down as they greeted her.

This time Sally handed each girl an envelope. They tore them open eagerly and again looked disappointed.

"You know, Auntie Sally," the little girl had her hands on her hips, "our other auntie buys us really nice things, expensive things, so that we have everything we want. We like her better."

The girls went off to play.

At Christmas, Sally came again for a visit. As usual, the twins asked what she had brought them.

"I brought you something very special," Sally said, pulling an envelope out of her purse. "Since your other auntie has given you everything you want, I've decided to give you something you need."

Sally opened the envelope and pulled out a piece of paper.

"This is a donation receipt. You've given a goat to a boy in Africa. He has no shoes, toys, or possibility of going to school. This gift will make his life and his family better."

The girls stared open-mouthed.

Sally smiled and continued, "What's more, he said thank you."

Cliff Hanger
Eileen Harris

It was Kiona's first free solo and onsite cliff climb. At this point in her climb, the precipice became more challenging.

Although the entire route had been above her technique level, Kiona knew that if she wanted to keep up with Stacey on future climbs, she had to improve quickly.

She took a breath in and fought to mantle herself upon a ledge. Her grip faltered. In response, she erred and glanced down. As she looked and realized she was going to fall thirty metres to the ground below, something grazed her wrist, and she panicked. She quickly jammed herself into the cliffside and squinted through her sweat to see—nothing.

Convincing herself it was probably some brush, Kiona slowly repositioned herself to take the ledge. Taking a few breaths, she felt muscle weakness setting in, but she could only go upwards.

As she found her foothold, she reached up with her right hand. Something restricted her wrist again, and she could not use her arm to reach the ledge above. The imbalance caused her other hand to slip, and she plummeted to the ground below, screaming as her limbs flailed. She had been so close!

Kiona felt a surge of anger swell inside her just before everything turned black. She ripped off the Virtual Reality headset and cursed.

She looked down to see that Stacey had grabbed her wrist to let her know that their time in the VR Zone was over.

Hello and Goodbye
Jackie Kierulf

"Hello, darling. You must be out enjoying yourself."

Nana often left that message for me.

Voicemail from her was bittersweet. It meant that when she called, she talked into space. It also meant that recording existed forever, even when I no longer would draw a breath.

She'd be settled in a pink recliner, one hand resting on the plush fabric, the other grasping the receiver. Her voice would be raised, intent on drowning out the television Grandpa played at top volume. The bombings during the war left him entirely deaf in one ear with only partial hearing in the other.

I punched in their number, eager to connect. Grandpa often joined us. As the line rang, I reminded myself to use my stage voice. Neither would notice, though.

"Oh, how lovely to hear from you!"

I knew her eyes were smiling. We spoke the day before, but that exchange was a thousand minutes ago. I hung onto every word we shared, and she did, too. Signing off, we never said goodbye but instead said, "Talk to you again."

I'm keeping vigil now. She has hours left.

Newly married and with my father away at sea, Mom depended on her. She welcomed me into the world, too. Now I dread being the last one to hang up, though that would be less painful than sitting at her bedside.

I swallow hard. My throat hurts. This time I'll hold on for as long as it takes.

You Grew Taller
Corina Hartley

You grew taller that night. More rugged and square. All without saying a word. You didn't need to, after all.

You waited so patiently, without complaint. Day after day, night after night. You gave your very soul to the quest of loving me. You did everything you could possibly muster to provide for me.

I need so much. I do not mean to, but I do. I warned you from the start, yet you signed up without hesitation. You took me in with all my flaws, fortitude, and feminine wiles. You chose me just as much as I chose you.

Yes, you held your ground that night. I was frightened. I was also intrigued. I liked to toy with you, taunt you, for my own selfish pleasure. Your jaw grew wider, your breath heavier, your stance unmoving as you stood behind me firmly, begging me to finish. I didn't want it to be over just yet, however.

The night was crisp, the sky starry, and the brisk breeze tickled my skin. I wanted to play longer and feel the dew forming on the grass as I ran from you.

"Catch me! Catch me!" I begged.

You grew weary of my games and gently smacked

my bare bottom. That's when I knew you meant business. It was now time to give you what you wanted.

With loving eyes, I stared up at you. Relief crossed your face markedly as you said, "Finally!" and got out the pooper scooper.

Winter Wind
Sally Quon

I listen to the wind rushing past the house, rattling windows and shaking shingles. The winds here are usually one of two kinds: the cold, arctic wind that comes out of the north, dangerous and biting, or the Chinook winds that come down from the mountains in the west, warm and dry, able to raise the temperature by thirty degrees in just a few hours.

Out here on the prairie, there's nothing between the wind and I except these four walls. There are no trees or buildings to buffer or block. The sound of the wind as it whistles and wails is one I've come to associate with home. The wind drifts and sculpts and polishes the ample snow. Entire roads can disappear without warning.

The cat stands at the patio door and meows. I open the door. She sniffs the air and shudders, giving me a look of disdain. Somehow, even though she considers herself the higher life form, the weather is under my control, and the fact that I won't change it for her is just rude. But never mind. In cold like this, the mice will come to her. In the meantime, let the wind blow. She returns to the fire and stretches out before it, comfortable and warm in her fur coat.

Yes, the fire looks very inviting. And is that the smell of soup coming from the kitchen? No? Well, it will be in an hour.

Risk
Elizabeth Buchan-Kimmerly

The door latch is broken, of course. It's been four years since The Event. All the canned goods are gone from the kitchen. Looted or eaten by the long-gone owners?

Hard to tell.

No one has lived here in months, maybe years. There's rat shit all over. The dog whines. Must be some rats still around. Someone took all the warm clothes and the blankets, too. For use or trade?

Hard to tell.

Looks like no one has taken the risk of going down into the cellar. The wooden stairs have collapsed into a pile of termite-ridden rot ten feet below the door. That could have been before The Event, though.

Hard to tell.

Drop a knotted rope down and another with a canvas duffel bag for whatever can be useful. A workbench offers rusty hammers and screwdrivers. Put them in the duffel. The power tools are useless, of course, but there would be some copper in the electric motors. Worth salvaging?

Hard to tell.

The dim light from dirty windows shows another

door and, behind it, a root cellar. With row upon row of home-canned fruit and tomatoes. Dust off the bottles. How long have they been here?

Hard to tell.

Fill the duffel and hoist them into the light. No signs of leakage, fermentation, or mold. How safe would they be to eat?

Hard to tell.

Try some on the dog. If she lives, we eat. If not, we eat her.

First Day of School
Eileen Harris

Stephanie Carson always had first-day jitters. Today was no different.

Her new high school was larger than she expected and surprisingly difficult to navigate. She wandered down each hall, glancing between her printed handout and the signs on the classroom doors. She had walked every hall and was now onto the last one.

"Can I help you get to your classroom?" a teacher asked. She wore a nametag with Mrs. Anne Smithers written on it.

Stephanie glanced down at her paper. "No, thank you, Anne. I think it's right here, actually."

Anne frowned. "It's Mrs. Smithers to you."

Stephanie mumbled an apology and hurried inside the classroom. She heaped her backpack and books onto the desk.

"What do you think you're doing?" Anne, or Mrs. Smithers, had followed her into the classroom. "This is grade twelve English. Are you sure you're supposed to be here?"

Stephanie checked her handout. The information indicated that she was in the right classroom, but

Anne's stare brought her uncertainty.

"Yes, I'm pretty sure," Stephanie replied hesitantly. Anne paused and curtly suggested that Stephanie move her items to a different location before she mumbled something about disrespect and today's youth.

Stephanie had always had trouble with being mistaken as younger. It appeared to have happened again.

She sighed and attached the nametag that read Ms. Carson to her shirt. Stephanie could only hope that the students wouldn't treat her, their new teacher, in the same manner.

The Farmer
Jo-Anne Johnson

The newborn's cry was cut short by a bolt to the head, and its body was tossed into the hover-barrow nearby. The container teetered on the brink of overflow.

"Almost full," he said as he turned his attention back to the task at hand—his mind lingering on the bodies in the hover-barrow for a breath.

Deftly, he attached the machines to 173's heavy breasts. A sigh escaped her, bordering on comprehensible. Did she just say *please*? He looked up. She stared at him with unsettling blue eyes. Her face was streaked with moisture leaking from them, and the rivulets left clean flushed skin in their wake.

Filthy creatures, he thought as he finished with the milking machine and moved toward the next stall.

"Please," she said again.

He turned to face her. She grasped the bars of her cage with white knuckles; her gaze still fixed on him. And for a moment, he wondered if the human rights activists were right. Could these creatures suffer?

He quickly dismissed the thought as the hover-barrow beeped an impatient warning that it had reached capacity, and a human scream rang out from the far end of the barn. Two hundred twenty-three must be in labour.

It was going to be a busy day, which meant a profitable day. And that was why he came here to Earth—the shithole of the galaxy—to make money.

He smiled as he made his way to 223's stall.

Hope
Christy Hartman

"Angel, I need you to be a big girl. When the car stops, unbuckle as fast as you can." Josie tilted her head so the little girl could see her through the rear-view mirror.

Angel nodded. A distant noise reminded her of the red fire truck where her dad worked. The car sped up as the sirens grew louder. Josie veered abruptly, throwing the little girl against the door.

"Now, Angel!" Josie shouted.

Angel fought with the booster seat as Josie threw open the door. She hoisted Angel onto her hip and ran towards the woods. She struggled with the weight of the little girl.

"I want my mommy." Angel clung to Josie's neck.

This was not part of the plan. Josie anticipated more time. Preschool pickup was easy with Angel's new nanny on the pick-up list. They simply walked out, holding hands, chatting about paper dolls and silly songs.

Beams of light suddenly lit up the forest. Blinded, Josie tripped. They tumbled hard to the ground. The stomach-turning sound of bones breaking bounced off the silent trees like a firecracker.

Josie held her little girl tightly, stroking brown curls that mirrored her own.

"I'm sorry, baby."

"I want my mommy." Angel's voice shook as she buried her face into Josie's chest.

"You'll be back with your mommy soon," Josie soothed.

The pounding footsteps reached them. Josie screamed with pain and defeat as hands yanked Angel from her arms, just as they had in the hospital five years earlier.

Sidestep
Mary Long-Shimanke

"I was talking to so and so about this the other day, and I pointed out to him that at least in Canada, we educated the Native people. Not like in the States," George said.

"Educated? What do you mean?"

"At residential schools."

I could have heeded the slight pressure of my husband tensing up beside me, but I heard my grandmother's voice whisper in my ear, "We haven't got all day."

The rest of the conversation is hard to recall. An awakening dragon had reared up, blocking the scene. It went something like this.

"You might want to stop now, George."

"Well, we did, Mary. We opened schools for them." His tone said eighty-year-old men are much more informed than sixty-year-old women.

"No, George, they were torn from their families. Some never went back home. Some died at those schools. For sure, they were abused."

Standing up, I took a breath. "It wasn't about education."

I heard a rage in my voice. I had so much more to say, but he left.

All he said was, "Oh." His electric golf cart silently glided across the grass. It was about erasing their culture. I screamed silently to his retreating back.

"I did it," I said to my husband, turning to face him. "I found my voice."

"You did," was all he said. He squeezed my hand.

We sat and watched the baby loons play just off the shore. I felt peace bloom up in my chest.

Fried Banana
Sally Quon

The kitchen was hot. Ivy's mind was numb, and she couldn't think straight. Three days of working night and day, partying in between, cocaine, no food, and no sleep, all catching up with her.

The drugs had worn off an hour ago, and it would be at least three hours before she could hook up with something more.

It was lunchtime. Her section was a mess. She hadn't taken coffee around for at least ten minutes. Someone somewhere had asked for their bill, but for the life of her, she couldn't remember who.

"Ivy!"

Ivy turned. It was the chef.

"What's up?"

"Mistake. Here, have this."

Ivy looked at the plate of fried bananas, vanilla ice cream, and caramel sauce. She didn't have time for this, but damn, it looked good. For a moment, she thought she might faint. Maybe one little bite. Ivy grabbed a fork and dug in.

Time stopped. Chaos erupted all around her, but she couldn't see or hear. All she knew was the taste, the texture of the warm, crispy banana and cool, sweet ice cream. Never had anything tasted so good.

She was incapable of caring about the fate of all those faceless customers until the last bite had been taken. Ivy sighed, silently blessed chef, and headed back out to see what could be salvaged from the lunch rush after her impromptu time-out.

"Time to straighten this mess out," she muttered, wondering if she meant her section or her life.

The Big Score
Eileen Harris

Tonight would be the night that Alyson would score with Brad. Alyson wasn't certain what she needed to do to make it happen, but her friends told her that boys loved makeup, so she snuck into her mother's bathroom and borrowed some.

She started with mascara, promptly poking herself in the eyes and causing them to water.

She turned on the crimper, cramming strands of hair between the metal plates. After burning her scalp, she gave up and teased her hair into a wild mane.

She looked at the time. Five minutes until Brad picked her up. She hastily applied red nail polish to her nails, cuticles, even sprinkling her knuckles.

She powdered on too much bright pink blush and coughed, but there was no time to remove anything. Finally, she smeared red lipstick across her lips.

A horn beeped. It was time to go. She raced past her mother on the stairs. Her mom gawked and started to speak, but Alyson had already grabbed her bag and left. She climbed into the van and greeted Brad cheerfully.

Brad looked over at her. "Uhhh …" was all he

said.

"Ready to go?" Brad's mom stifled a giggle as her eyes met Alyson's in the mirror.

Alyson didn't notice and cheerfully replied, "Yes, Mrs. A! All set. Got my hockey gear and stick. Brad and I are definitely going to score tonight!"

Off they went to the hockey arena to play in the big game.

Cell Phone Widow
Diane Rudolph

If life's what happens between texts, notice how we flit from village to medieval village at kamikaze speeds between fields of sunflowers that nod in one direction. Sections of them are missing heads leaving only stalks.

We stop at a restaurant next to a gas station. The heat is combative. A chorus of cicadas chant. Sweat forms and trickles, but I prefer it to the dishonesty of air conditioning.

He cringes at the dusty plastic chairs on the patio and sits. He glares at the farmer man standing at the railing who smokes and coughs. The farmer sends phlegm into the bushes with the precision of a blow-dart. I chuckle.

Our waitress speaks no English. He hasn't attempted Catalan in weeks. Thankfully, it's a set menu of gazpacho, squid, potatoes, and wine.

He begins his daily ritual of deleting old photos to free up space for new ones. He doesn't trust the cloud. A hornet lands on his shoulder. I say nothing. Like when he's driving in the wrong direction and insists he isn't.

The coughing man glances at me apologetically.

I smile.

He perks up when the meal arrives, which is delicious. The wine settles me.

"What do you suppose happens to insomniacs during siesta?" I savour the gazpacho.

He ignores me.

"Do you think they hunt vampires in the caves?"

But he has decapitated himself. I'm a cell phone widow again.

As the fine cold soup plumps every molecule of my being, I decide to leave him.

Pigeon Post
Marlene Lewis

Andrea walked out to the loft with grain for her pigeons. She owned eight racing homing pigeons, five veterans, and three first-year flyers.

Of her veterans, Walter was her favorite, not because he was a top winner in competition but because he had bonded with her in an extraordinary way.

As she stepped into the loft, she clicked and whistled, calling her birds to dinner. She scanned the perches as each pigeon flew down to the feeder.

Something was wrong. Walter was missing.

Andrea continued to click and whistle as she searched the entire loft and aviary for Walter. She put out clean water and went back to the house.

Shaking and near panic, Andrea tried to think. No furry or feathered predator could get to her pigeons—her loft was too well built. Had Walter been stolen? What could a thief do with a highly recognizable Janssen racing pigeon? The racing community knew Walter. She needed to call her dearest friend, Ned.

He'd have some ideas. Just then, Andrea heard cooing and shuffling in the loft. Running outside, she saw Walter drop into the trap and disappear inside. She slipped into the loft and cradled Walter in her hands, surprised to see a tiny harness strapped to his chest with a box attached. How strange, she thought. Andrea carefully opened the box, and a diamond ring fell out, along with a note.

Walter and I love you, but I'm the one who wants to marry you. Ned.

The Following
Elaine Jameson

The emerald trees covered the area. The Beings nestled on their ledges, extending from the brown rockery alcove they had lived in for three thousand years.

They moved their giraffe-like heads side to side in seamless rhythm, and the forest shimmered and came alive with powerful energy.

The WisdomHolder raised his hoof while straightening his long, freckled neck, then rotated his ears first to listen and then to capture the shimmers.

Each capture of energy burned through him like electricity, waving through his giraffe-like lips, a buzzing crescendo. It was musical, penetrating.

The Beings received the shivery message from the buzzing, and each began to hum in unison. The humming meant that something important was about to occur.

YoungBrightOne looked around and wondered what would happen if he were to disobey the message.

If he opposed what was being suggested, would WisdomHolder cast him out? He had heard the stories of the Murky Middle.

It was cold and dark with no music or joy. It was

where the Disobedients were sent. No one had ever come back, not even his father.

He heard the message in his head once again. There was a shifting of feet and an excitement to move. He tried to think of a response but faltered. All he could think of was The Others and the responsibility.

"If The Others are removed, The Beings will hold the loss."

All Beings turned towards him, feet crunching. They waited for orders in death-like silence.

One Last Ride
Corina Hartley

He paced a trench into the cement with his Doc Martins. He wouldn't let her die. No permission given. Nada. To say goodbye would be the end, and he didn't care if it was selfish. He would do anything for her, at any cost.

Test after test, the diagnosis was clear yet still too painful to accept. His guilt overrode all his senses until he couldn't even think straight. This crash would be the last.

He was losing her, yet he refused to let her go alone. One last ride, just the two of them. Yes, that was it.

"We'll do this together, baby. Just you and me. Won't you purr one last time for me?"

He crouched as low to the ground as he could and used all his strength to pick her up and set her straight. To stand with dignity, even if one last time.

Her life's blood spilled onto the open road, and he knew he had to act fast. He breathed life into her for what he knew would be the last time. He cranked up the tunes as they rode like lovers do into the dark abyss.

***

Stratton hats to their chest, the boys in blue gave their deepest condolences to his Mrs. later that night.

"I told him to flush her brake fluid. He shouldn't have listened to her. Now he will be buried with that stupid bike of his while I sip margaritas on the beach with his insurance money."

Mojave Mambo
Jan Manchur

Dust raged out from the tires spinning on the sandy track. Funny, after all these years, I'd want to go back, right to the exact spot. The journey is like a nail, which is me, to a magnet, which is you.

I jumped out of the truck and grabbed my supplies from the back. Heat shimmered in the distance like a ghost you couldn't quite see.

A drink. That's what I need. The folding chair slid into the sliver of shade from the Joshua tree. I dropped my things and plopped into the chair. Sweat trickled down the gap in my bra. I pressed my hand to my T-shirt, mopping it up.

There's no refinement to Cuervo's finest in a plastic cup. No salt. No lime. I belted it back. It burned all the way down. There didn't used to be a reason to drink.

Shot number two tumbled down easier. I watched a horny toad pose stiff-legged in the sand. Here we are. Just you and me and the lizard.

Shot number three dulled reality. I picked up the shovel.

Your bone marked the sand like a plow on my bleary pilgrimage back to the truck. I crumpled, holding you in my arms. It wasn't supposed to be like this. It should have been love.

I'm shackled to this place for all time. Before leaving, I shove that bone back down to hell. Back down to hell where I belong.

A Nice Cup of Tea
Debby Vollbrecht

Hazel rummaged through her bags, grumbling, then slumped onto the courtyard bench, resigned to the empty day ahead. She brightened as she watched Emily struggle out the door, Kaylee and stroller in tow.

A cheery "Morning, Hazel," and they were gone.

Tsk! Careless girl forgot to lock up again.

Hazel rose, knees creaky. Tea time.

The floral teapot with matching cup was her favourite. A little milk, a dollop of sugar, hot black tea.

She helped herself to a cookie, then shuffled into the living room and eased onto the recliner. She dipped her cookie in the tea and gummed it down. She slurped noisily, smacking her lips. Then, tea finished, she put her tired feet up and snoozed.

Hazel snorted awake. Time to tidy up before heading out.

She washed and dried the cup and spoon, rinsed the teapot, and put them away. She tossed the teabag into the compost bin and wiped the counter.

She used the toilet, then washed with scented soap, enjoying the warm suds on her old hands. She wiped the sink bowl with toilet paper and flushed.

Unlike Emily, Hazel was careful.

Next week, another young woman joined Emily and Kaylee on their outing.

"Morning, Hazel."

Hazel offered her toothless grin.

Emily mouthed to her friend, "Homeless," nodding at Hazel's bags piled high on the cart.

"Did you lock up?" the friend whispered.

"Oh! I always forget." Emily skipped back and locked the door.

Pity, Hazel thought. I'd have liked a nice cup of tea.

Rest Area Intrigue
Theresa Leinemann

After a long day traveling in northern BC, we pulled into a rest area off the highway. A sign advised our stay to be less than eight hours. Our exhaustion warranted a decent sleep and was worth the risk of a stern reprimand, fine, or prison time.

In the morning, refreshed and ready to endure another long day of traveling, I opened the blinds. A fair-sized sapling now spanned the exit, and a truck had stopped, unable to enter the rest area. The driver exited the vehicle, glanced at our motor home with what I perceived as a suspicious look, then moved the tree to the side.

The truck drove past a BC provincial park vehicle according to the logo on the door and parked by the bathrooms. Would they think we placed the tree there, city folk fearful of unsavoury characters preying on unsuspecting travelers during the night?

I wanted to explain our situation, begging forgiveness for overstaying our welcome. They didn't look like they cared.

We were in the middle of the wilderness, a few minutes from the highway. Why would someone place a tree across the road trapping us?

After a speedy breakfast, we headed out, puzzled but free to continue our journey without confrontation. As we passed the fallen tree, a jagged stump beside the road showed unmistakable signs of the real culprit. It was nature's industrious carpenter, the majestic beaver doing what comes naturally in the middle of a forest, far away from civilization.

Sudden Storm
Ann Tiplady

I said, "I'm going to check the cows."

"I'll come too," John said.

Normally I would have checked them in the afternoon, but I was running late. It was early evening, and the lowering sun made a lovely, glowing, yellow light. We would walk.

We could see the cows down at the end of the long field, where it rose to a knoll with a copse of sugar maples on top. They liked it there.

As we approached, I called out my usual "Hi cows, hi," so they would know it was me and not take fright. They looked at us and continued chewing cud. Their water was clean and fresh, the fences were good, and they were content.

We turned back towards the house. Huge black clouds were boiling over the nearby ridge that ran along the west side of the field. Thunder rumbled low and loud. Suddenly we were out in a dangerous electrical storm.

"We need to run!" I said.

"I can't," John said.

I abandoned him, apologizing but running ahead.

We needed to separate. Our kids were still young, and if lightning were to strike, we needed only one of us to be killed.

I struggled through the long grass, past the crumpled cherry tree that had exploded spirally when lightning struck in an earlier storm.

I made it to the house, chest heaving. John arrived shortly after. I don't know if he forgave me for leaving him behind.

But I had to. Right?

Fate
Christy Hartman

"Shell, how'd I let you talk me into this?" Lynne paused to apply another coat of mascara to her lashes. "Do you even know this guy?"

Shelby fluffed her feathered hair in the mirror and looked back at her friend.

"Tom's fantastic, a real looker. Plus, he's Gerry's best friend. You'll get along great."

Gerry and Shelby were steady for two months already. She was anxious for their friends to meet.

Lynne couldn't understand what Shelby saw in Gerry. Unruly red hair and dark horn-rimmed glasses were not the Marlon Brando look Shelby usually went for. His skin was freckled and sun-browned from summer work on the family farm.

The diner buzzed with families and teenagers. Tom held the door, complimented her new dress, and made conversation. The group chatted and laughed about small-town gossip while they waited for their burgers and shakes.

Lynne's painted fingertips reached the Heinz bottle as his calloused hand curled around it. The universe narrowed and paused in the space between their fingertips. Blue eyes met hazel. Eternity lasted less than a second. He knew. She knew.

The three dropped Lynne at home with waves and promises to repeat the evening. She stayed on the porch, hands in her lap, a small smile on her lips, a betrayal of the plans being formed. A sparkling ring. A white dress. Pink sleeping babies. Fingers intertwined.

His Buick pulled up to the sidewalk. Gerry silently joined her on the swing. "How am I going to tell Shelby?"

Dumpster Dave
Sally Quon

His name is Dumpster Dave. He's in his early fifties but looks much older with his long, wild hair and unkempt beard.

Dave smells so bad that I find myself holding my breath when he talks to me. I am certain Dave's smell has less to do with uncleanliness (although he's not the cleanest person) and more to do with malnutrition. He is the definition of gaunt.

Dave just is. He is one of those people who exist on the fringes of civilization. People cross the street to avoid having to walk past him. He's never been anywhere or done anything. He just survives.

What most people don't know about Dave is that he grew up in a Salvation Army Orphanage. He's never had a family, never known love. Dave saved up his money, and on his birthday, he took his friends to Swiss Chalet for lunch. His friends are a small collection of stuffed animals.

Whenever I see Dave, he says, "Give the kids a kiss for me!"

I always say, "I will, Dave."

But I don't. The truth is, I don't want my kids to

know about the existence of people like Dave.

I don't shelter my kids from much. They've seen hookers and addicts in their own neighbourhood at night. But to know about someone like Dave, whose only crime was to be born into a world that couldn't even offer him love, is just too sad.

A Renaissance Studio
Marlene Lewis

"Lisa, thou art late!"

"I must needs have my comestio before sitting here, Nardo. Prosecco and la tortiera."

"Thou must needs be here when I require. The light, the light!"

"This attic presses on me."

"This studio is situated ideally for the light from the north. I need to paint."

"How much longer need I sit?"

"Until I am finished."

"How much longer?"

"Thou, cara, are simply a bowl of fruit, a mountain, a cow. Thou art an impassive model and ergo have no use other than as an object for me to observe and reproduce on this wood panel. A bowl of fruit is blessedly silent."

"Thou, Nardo, art a pig. I will complain to Francesco that thou mistreat me!"

"Francesco desires this portrait of thee, although only the buon Dio in Heaven and Francesco know why. I would rather paint a cow for him to idolize. Sit still!"

Dribbles, Drabbles, and Postcards

"This chair is hard. I need a soft cushion."

"Thou seem'st to carry thy own cushion behind thee. Too much tortiera. Move thy hands to the left to cover that prosecco stain."

"Have a care, Nardo, that I do not tell Il Duca what I know about that dinner thou painted for him on Santa Maria's wall."

"Thou wouldst not!"

"I wouldst."

"Here is a cushion for you, cara."

"And . . .?"

"Now what, cara Lisa?"

"I am not a cow."

"Thou art not a cow."

"And . . .?"

"And I adore thee, carissima!"

Then Mona smiled.

Come Play with Me
By: Marlene Lewis

Hettie sat motionless on a bench in Vienna's Kunsthistoriches Museum. She was mesmerized by the huge painting in front of her: "Children's Games," painted by Pieter Bruegel in 1560.

She had no idea why her parents decided to take her with them on a tour of Europe's famous museums. Now that she was twelve, she could have stayed at home in Atlanta with the next-door neighbour looking in on her every so often.

Hettie was a short, round girl, not pretty but by no means ugly. Round face, round hands, round feet, round body. She'd never had friends, which was fine with her. She accepted the fact that she'd never fit in anywhere. So why would her parents want her with them in this lovely world of art and beauty?

Hettie's eyes were bright as they roamed over the canvas, eagerly studying the hundreds of village children playing games, some she recognized and others she didn't. They were all having so much fun. The museum brochure slipped out of her hand onto the bench.

In another room of the museum, Hettie's parents

pondered Vermeer's "The Art of Painting," intrigued by its details and lighting technique. Reluctant to leave, Hettie's mother sighed, "We should look for Hettie, I guess."

They wandered into the Bruegel gallery and saw a museum brochure lying on the empty bench. Standing in front of the painting, they searched among the laughing children.

"There she is." Hettie's father pointed. "She looks happy now."

Hard to Understand
Elaine Jameson

Lilith impatiently peered into the office.

"Miss Nurse Mauve! Can I have my pop, please?" Lilith called. Mauve bustled into sight and smiled forcibly, all teeth, no eyes.

"Of course, Lilith. How are you? Any visitors coming?"

"No, why would anyone come?" Lilith became anxious.

"Oh, just wondering." Mauve handed Lilith the drink. Lilith took off the tab, handing it to Mauve. Nurses did not want dangerous, little metal pieces drifting around the ward. Lilith covered her wrist with her sleeve.

"Well. I've been here nine weeks and in that time not one visitor. Not one. So I got nervous." Lilith explained, trying to be polite.

"Okay, now go get some sun in the dayroom. Get some rest and enjoy your pop." Mauve sing-songed and slinked into the back room.

Lilith saw Renae sitting in the dayroom. She sat. Renae stared at the TV blankly. Lilith wished certain people could understand the immense humiliation of being placed in Westwinds Psychiatric Unit. Yet, the nurses seemed to think this was a day camp.

Renae caught Lilith's attention and offered her the shiny metal piece in her hand. Renae smirked victoriously. She made a sawing motion on her wrist and grinned.

Lilith deliberated, stunned. She knew if she took it, Renae would think they were friends. If she didn't, she was giving Renae permission to hurt herself. Lilith felt slightly ill and stood up.

"No judgement," she said. "I think we are here to try to make our life worth living."

The Cabin
Sharlene McNeill

I went camping on this beautiful mountain, but the weather was terrible. I can't pitch my tent. I feel flustered. Everything is sludge. All my supplies are ruined. So, I walk up the hill and spy a cabin.

It's rundown, and the wood is rotten, but I take my chances. The door opens, and I'm now safe from the onslaught of wind, hail, and snow.

I find wood and tinder to strike a fire. Then, I hear a mewling cry above the echo of the pelting rain. So, I open the door to a great gasp of cold air.

On the porch is a brave little kitten. I suspect that a cat has given birth underneath the porch. I make a bed for this kitten.

But I still need to get the mother cat and her kittens to come inside. I look through my backpack to see what foods I can offer.

I find a tin of tuna to coax the cat inside. The fire I made is going strong and keeps the inside of the cabin comfortable. So, I open the door and put the tuna on the deck. It works, but she's wary of me.

I'm okay with them being feral. We are all uncomfortable strangers enjoying the warmth of the fire. We are here for necessity and not because we like each other. It's better than being alone.

I'll keep the fire going and watch over the cats. I'll sip tea until the weather settles down.

Academic Priorities
Stevi Stephens

There is a saying, "To keep your wife, keep her pregnant and barefoot." However, I was both when I left my husband.

The village pigs had devoured my left sandal. The pigs adored me and constantly monitored me as a consistent food source since my morning sickness lasted twenty-four hours and I tended to barf often.

My archaeologist husband was not sympathetic, declaring that "morning sickness was a culturally constructed psychological problem." So, when he headed up the coast of Papua to inspect the pottery in a cursed cave, I broke into our patrol chest, extracted my ticket back to Canberra, took some money, and I hitchhiked to Port Moresby on a Mission Air Flight.

I was a pitiful sight when I reached Canberra. Shoes were required by the airlines, so I now wore rubber flip-flops. My shift dresses were mildewed, and I had lost more than two stone (28 pounds) due to pregnancy and malaria. All of our possessions were stored in Brian's office at the university. These included much needed clean clothes, real shoes, and a ticket back to the USA.

As I was sorting through our suitcases, I was approached by one of Brian's doctoral committee members. "I gather that you are leaving your husband."

I affirmed that was, indeed, the case. To my surprise, he responded most strongly with, "Oh, but you can't do that!"

"Why not?" I asked.

"Because we never had you to dinner."

The Sale
Anne Minnings

"Stupid cow, do I have to explain how to do everything?" Claymore's voice dripped with contempt.

"Sorry, sorry." Janet twisted her fingers together and looked at the ground.

"We're so done." Claymore went on. "Sell the Miata. I've told you how to do it. Here's the signed paperwork for my end. I think I've made it all perfectly clear."

"How much should I ask for it?"

"Just get it sold," he growled. "I'll be back in town next week, and when I call you, you'd better have the money for me."

Janet dutifully placed an ad for the Miata. There were immediate responses from several prospective buyers. The first one to show up could have the car. She didn't want to have to explain to Claymore if the car hadn't sold.

Claymore called the following week and directed Janet to meet him at a coffee shop downtown.

He was already there when she arrived. He didn't ask if she'd like to order anything or even to sit down. He just held out his hand.

"Here's the paperwork and the cash." She handed him an envelope as she spoke and then turned toward the door.

"What the bloody hell?" Claymore's voice had risen a full octave. "There's only a hundred here. That car was worth at least twenty thousand!"

"Oh?" Janet paused in the doorway. "I guess you didn't make quite everything perfectly clear."

Then she turned and shut the door behind her as she stepped out into the sun.

Silent Reverie
Cathy Airth

One rainy spring day, Adelaide's husband was digging up muddy potatoes when he felt a sharp numbing pain that dropped him to the ground. His body turned cold as he grasped at the dirt.

He sunk face down, unable to move, unable to stop from sucking mud into his mouth and nose. From time to time, he mounted a rally by rolling his head sideways above the sludge that rose and seeped into his mouth. His efforts pushed his face deeper into the dirt as he lost leverage. He died face down as the mud dried in his nostrils and his matted hair.

That's how Adelaide found him. She saw a strange shadow in the field. As she got closer to it, she tried to guess what it was—a dog, a piece of wood, a peaked furrow—but deep within her, she knew what and who it was. As she approached him, her heart beat harder and faster. When she saw him, it slowed and steadied.

She had never seen anyone dead before. Long shadows flickered on the ground. It was almost dark when Adelaide finally pulled herself out of her silent reverie.

She was cold, and her muscles were stiff when she

arrived at her parents' farm. Her father opened the door, but she spoke only to her mother, saying flatly, "He's dead in the field."

After a long but deliberate pause, her mother replied, "You know, there will need to be another husband."

The Game
Debby Vollbrecht

If you're reading this, I must be dead.

Her fingers traced the words that started the game.

My God, how he'd latched on to that idea! They'd watched this movie, and he couldn't stop yammering on about how, if he uncovered a crime and the perps knew it, he'd leave just such a document with his lawyer.

He called it his game and worked out the details non-stop—at the breakfast table, the dinner table. He turned into a regular Walter Mitty.

Well, she could play the game, too. She staged little incidents. She hired a private detective to follow him, so he'd notice and suspect the fantasies were real. She became addicted to the game, thrilled with the feeling of power. She encouraged his fears and thrashed over the dangers with him at dinner and in bed.

Should he call the cops? Would they take him seriously?

No evidence, she commiserated.

His enthusiastic intrigues turned into paranoid delusions. He knew he'd witnessed something somewhere, but what? He racked his brain and replayed his days step by step. How could a tell-all document protect him if he had nothing to tell?

He lost his appetite, couldn't sleep, and aged ten years. He started to screw up at work.

He believed work harboured his enemy and threatened to quit.

She decided it was time to end this and protect the pension.

A week later, it was all over.

Her hand lingered over the inscription.

She smiled as she left the cemetery.

An anthology of short, short stories

Author Biographies

Airth, Cathy

Cathy Airth taught Literature and Essay Writing for many years at the university level. She obtained a BA and an MA from the University of Alberta, where she was a PhD Candidate and where she won the Graduate Teaching Award. Her short story "Silent Reverie" is a shortened version of the prologue to her first novel, Osithe. The book traces the history of several generations of women struggling to make their way in a world not for them.

Agustín, Nelson

Nelson Agustín is a non-binary graphic designer, fine art photographer, and writer. Their alphabet book, *A for Adobo*, was published by Tahanan Books in 2010. They independently published their first collection of flash fiction, *The Door Knockers, and Other Stories*, on Amazon in 2022.

Boghean, Sue

The best years of Sue's life were raising her sons. Now that their children are raised, and her husband has passed, she's metamorphosing. She no longer cares about working long hours. She wants to write. She describes herself as a beginner with everything to learn and can hardly wait.

Brown, Marilyn J.

Marilyn has lived in Kelowna for twenty-five years. Previously, she was a regularly published contributor to *Beyond 50* seniors' magazine for seven years and had an eclectic blog (cubbyholewriter.com) of her humorous take on life. She is currently working on a collection of entertaining anecdotes entitled *Blue Sky Holes*.

Brown, P. F.

P. F. Brown has been writing poems and stories of late. Her first expressive outlet is painting, but she has been interested in exploring the written word for some time. This is an exciting new chapter in her creative life.

Buchan-Kimmerly, Elizabeth

Retired to Vancouver Island after forty years in Ottawa, her first published piece was "The Homestead Goat" for Agriculture Canada in 1969. Her most recent publication was "October 1954" in Stellar Evolutions, 2020. She has three unpublished novels, two being polished, one unpublishable. She has never met a goat.

Carr, Fern G. Z.

Fern, a member of the League of Canadian Poets and the Federation of BC Writers, and composes poetry in six languages, including Mandarin. Published worldwide and the recipient of several honours, Carr is thrilled her poetry is in orbit around the planet Mars aboard NASA'S MAVEN spacecraft. (ferngzcarr.com)

Cavouras, Anna

Anna finds stories everywhere. Some appear in *Studio Magazine, Boneyard Soup*, and the *League of Canadian Poets*. She is a former writer-in-residence with Firefly Creative Writing. Currently, she is a judge with Reedsy Prompts and an editorial assistant with Minerva Rising Press. She always carries her feminist agenda. @a.cavouras.writer

Clifton, Kristi

Kristi Clifton writes for children, most recently working on *The Adventures of MathaMax* series. Her publications for BC schools include a series of rhymes and chants for oral language development, and several non-fiction guided reading books. Writing for grown-ups is a new undertaking, spurred on by tranquil walks on Vancouver Island beaches during the pandemic.

Corps, Tess

Tess Corps writes from her cottage in British Columbia, Canada. She's been around the world and loves riding her Harley Davidson through the mountains near her home. Tess unearthed her passion for writing when she published her first non-fiction novel: *Trusting the Journey*. She publishes article submissions related to life experiences and writes copy for companies to improve their product exposure.

Gugin Maddex, Elaine

Elaine Gugin Maddex grew up in Minnedosa, Manitoba, following her grandmother around her massive gardens. Elaine is an author and kitchen herbalist who enjoys concocting new remedies, growing herbs, working on her books, and spending time with family and friends. *More Than a Wise Woman, Wise Woman's Manor, Wise Woman's Homage*, and *The Magick of New Beginnings* are available on Amazon.

Harris, Eileen

Eileen is a consistent contradiction. She is an extroverted introvert who enjoys intentionally partaking in random acts of rational creativity. She currently lives with her husband and child in beautiful BC, Canada.

Hartley, Corina

Corina Hartley is a storyteller who finds joy in nature walks and feeding forest birds from her hands. Her biggest mission in life is to love in the moment, one being at a time. She is a practicing dental hygienist who writes for fun and vows to publish sub-genre romance novels one day.

Hartman, Christy
Christy Hartman is a retail manager in Comox, British Columbia, and has an English literature degree from the University of British Columbia.

Jackson, Maggie
Maggie Jackson lives in Victoria, BC, near the ocean. She loves to go there daily, smell the fresh air, and dig for treasures. In the winter months, she loves to sit by the fire and dream up interesting stories.

Jameson, Elaine
Elaine lives in Vernon, BC with her family. She is thankful for the land and beauty they live on, which is the traditional land of the Sylyx people of the Okanagan. She had several poetry pieces published and some newspaper articles. Elaine works in a youth mental health program as a registered psychiatric nurse. In order to maintain her well-being, she takes writing courses and paints.

Johnson, Jo-Anne
When Jo-Anne isn't dreaming up ways to make science fiction and fantasy cruelty-free, she hides in the

mountains of Alberta, looking for forest fires. She is currently seeking representation for her debut novel, *Pig*.

Kierulf, Jackie

Jackie is from Ottawa, Ontario, Canada. Her publications include "The Bluff" (Paddler Press), "Saturday" (Route 7 Review), "Forgiven" (Tidbits), "Baking Lessons" (Williams Lake Tribune, BC, Canada), and "The Father I Knew" (Grief Dialogues). Besides writing, Jackie enjoys hiking, reading, and traveling. cherishingthedeathprocess.wordpress.com and fromsimplewordstorealstories.home.blog.

Kishchuk, Nat

Nat began writing fiction a couple of years ago after decades of doing something else completely. She has published one story in *Carte Blanche* and is grateful to live and work in Tiohtià:ke (Montréal), on the traditional, unceded territory of the Kanien'kehá:ka people.

Lancaster, Sharon

Sharon Lancaster houses a treasure chest of memories and ideas. She grew up on military bases worldwide, settling in Canada as a young adult. She calls Kelowna her home but is a pilgrim at heart. A soulful traveller with a gift for seeing the extraordinary in the ordinary, she lives life with passion and intention. (SharonLancaster.com)

Leinemann, Theresa

Theresa has self-published four fiction novels under the name T.A. Leinemann. *Arcadia Deception, Flight Control (sequel to Arcadia Deception), Tess,* and *Hidden Gems*. Her award-winning short story, *When Nature Calls,* is on her website, (taleinemann.wordpress.com), where she wrote about their RV adventures. She and her husband recently became grandparents, which she calls her greatest adventure yet.

Lewis, Marlene

Marlene Lewis retired to Washington's Olympic Peninsula after forty-six years in Alaska. She writes personal essays and short fiction and has introduced and annotated the 1867 play *Alaska, A Spectacular Extravaganza in Rhino-Russian Rhyme and Two Acts*. Marlene taught English at the University of Alaska and Wayland Baptist University and is currently working on a historical novel.

Long-Shimanke, Mary

Mary is a sixty-ish-something reluctant writer. She started taking writing courses a few years ago. She and her husband now live on Vancouver Island. Her two adult daughters, who both live in BC, tolerate her. Her two grandchildren tolerate her slightly more. She has a couple of pieces published in online literary magazines.

McNeill, Sharlene

A passionate visual storyteller, Sharlene delights in bringing the author's tale to life. Her earliest and fondest memories are those of standing in her back garden in front of an easel and reading books with her mother. She currently writes for personal pleasure and illustrates children's books.

Manchur, Jan

Jan is a retired English and drama teacher. She doesn't usually write wild stories like the one she submitted. It came out of a writing exercise some years ago. She was shortlisted for the Cedric Awards in 2016. Jan has also won a few contests and been published in local magazines.

Minnings, Anne

After retiring from a career with the BC government, Anne joined a couple of non-profit boards as treasurer and volunteers with her professional association, the Chartered Professional Accountants of BC. She lives in Victoria with her cat and her husband, close to their two daughters and families.

Nybo, Darcy

Darcy Nybo has published four children's books, two collections of short stories and a metaphysical novel. She is a word nerd who loves to help others succeed. Darcy is a multiple award-winning author, a sought-after book and magazine editor, and writing coach/instructor. She owns alwayswrite.ca and artisticwarrior.com. When she's not reading or writing, she's with her family, gardening, or painting.

Pawlik, Kelly

Kelly Pawlik dabbled with story writing from a young age. She spent her childhood reading, dressing up her beloved cat, Midnight, in doll clothes, and hunting garter snakes in the backyard. Kelly is the author of the Olympic Vista Chronicles (olympicvistapublishing.com), a middle-grade series set in the eighties that's suitable for all ages.

Platts-Fanning, Jennifer

Jennifer Platts-Fanning is a recipient of a 2022 Island Literary Poetry Award, a 2020 Island Literary Short Story Award, the 2022 Battle Tales VII Champion, 2nd place winner of the *Humans of the World* 2022 Summer Poetry Challenge and published in the *White Wall Review* and *Write Launch* literary magazines.

Quon, Sally

Sally is a back-country blogger, dirt-road diva, and teller of tales. She was a finalist in the Vallum Chapbook Contest for two consecutive years. Her work has appeared in numerous anthologies, including *Better Left Standing*, Catlin Press 2022. Sally is an associate member of the League of Canadian Poets.

Ragaire, Hazel

Only ideas outnumber the books in Hazel's home. Breathing life into monster monstrosities and the just plain weird with a dash of horror or a sprinkle of sci-fi is what she does. Find her past, present, and future works at hazelragaire.com or @HRagaire on Twitter.

Rebrec, Angela

Angela is a multidisciplinary artist whose most recent work has appeared in *Vallum, Prairie Fire,* and *GRAIN*, as well as the anthology *Voicing Suicide* (Ekstasis Editions, 2020). Her 2020 collaboration with composer Mickie Wadsworth for ART SONG LAB has been included in *NewMusicShelf's Anthology of New Music for Trans & Nonbinary Voices, vol.1*. Angela's poetry films have received awards at the Barcelona International Film Festival, FilmmakerLife Awards, and Phoenix Shorts, among others. She lives on the unceded lands of the Coast Salish peoples.

Reilly, Katherine

By day she teaches; by night, Katherine loves spinning speculative tales, and her rescue mutts Savvie and Roxyrazzamatazz hear all the stories first. Find poetic adventures in *Shadow Atlas, Last Girls Club, Blink Ink*, and fiction published by Tree and Stone, Elly Blue Publishing, and Oddity Prodigy Productions. @ katecanwrite

Robinson, Kathy

Kathy lives near Victoria, BC, and spent thirty years as a teacher before turning her pen to creative work. She loves whimsical stories that bring levity to life. Currently, she's writing a young adult novel, *Crystals Among Us*, and enjoys jamming with friends (music therapy), gardening (dirt therapy), and travelling.

Rudolph, Diane

Dianne Rudolf is an emerging writer who lives in beautiful Ladysmith, British Columbia.

Rule, Michele

Michele Rule is a disabled poet and writer from Kelowna, BC. She is especially interested in the topics of chronic illness, relationships, and nature. Michele is published in *OYEDrum, Five Minute Lit, Pocket Lint, WordCityLit*, the anthologies *Spring Peepers and Poets for Ukraine*, and others. Her first chapbook is *Around the World in Fifteen Haiku*. She lives with a sleepy dog, two cats, and a fantastic partner.

Scott, Larry

Larry is the author of a humorous novel, *The Duckling House*, and lives in Victoria. He does volunteer gardening at a downtown church, where many unusual things turn up in the flower beds, compliments of night visitors who leave souvenirs behind.

Seabrook, Kara

Kara Seabrook recently graduated from Redeemer University with an Honours Bachelor of Arts with a focus on writing. She grew up in the country outside Hamilton, Ontario, with her parents, two brothers, and the family dog Kasey. Today, Kara continues to strengthen her craft as a storyteller.

Smith, Kathy A.

Before embarking on fiction writing, Kathy A. Smith authored over 250 non-fiction articles in over thirty publications on the subjects of business, health, and marine shipping.

Her work has appeared in *Reader's Digest*, *Times Colonist*, *Schizophrenia Digest*, and *Business Examiner*. She authored monthly columns for *Health Care News* and *Pacific Maritime Magazine*. kathywritesromance.com

Stephens, Dr. Margaret Editha
aka Stevi Stephens

Stevi Stephens is a retired anthropologist with field experience in the Canadian Arctic and Papua New Guinea. Raised to be a southern belle in the USA, she rebelled and came to Canada as a war resister.

She taught in colleges and universities without tenure from the age of twenty-three. Despite being a terrible single parent, her two children raised themselves to be marvelous productive adults.

Stone, Rania

Rania Stone is the author of five novels and eleven children's stories. She's a well-known author in Greece and has recently translated several of her novels into English. She's been writing for over two decades and calls Greece her home.

Tiplady, Ann

Ann is a Canadian-American-Canadian writer, biologist, former farmer, and almost economist. She writes memoirs, personal essays, non-fiction stories, and book reviews. When not at her desk, she is in her garden. anntiplady.com

Vollbrecht, Debby

Debby Vollbrecht retired to Sidney, BC, after a thirty-year career in adult education, having taught at both Yukon College, Whitehorse, and Capilano University, North Vancouver. In 2020, she self-published a novel, *A Cold Place for Secrets: A Yukon Mystery*, and is currently working on her second.

Acknowledgements

A big thank you to everyone who submitted their stories to this anthology. This book would not exist without you.

To the tireless judges who read each and every submission, know this book is here because of your unbiased and honest feedback. Audrey Magnusson, Nelson Armstrong, and Cat Rymerson did a fabulous job choosing which stories were included for your enjoyment.

I also want to thank Jonas Saul and Imagine Press Inc. (imaginepress.org) for proofreading the final copy.

Lastly, I thank you, the readers. Without you, writers wouldn't have any reason to bravely share their stories with you and the world.

An anthology of short, short stories